My Little Brother

David McPhail

Harcourt, Inc.

Orlando Austin New York San Diego Toronto London

For Deborah—
Hey, it was all her idea, anyway
—D. M.

www.HarcourtBooks.com

Illustrations colored by John O'Connor

Library of Congress Cataloging-in-Publication Data
McPhail, David, 1940–
My little brother/written and illustrated by David McPhail.
p. cm.
Summary: A boy describes all the things that he does not like about
having a younger brother—and the things he does like.
[1. Brothers—Fiction.] I. Title.
PZ7.M2427My 2004
[E]—dc21   2003007716
ISBN 0-15-204900-2

First edition

A C E G H F D B

Manufactured in China

The illustrations in this book were done in pen and ink
and hand colored with watercolors.
The display type was set in Fontesque Bold.
The text type was set in Memphis Medium.
Color separations by Bright Arts Ltd., Hong Kong
Manufactured by South China Printing Company, Ltd., China
This book was printed on totally chlorine-free Stora Enso Matte paper.
Production supervision by Sandra Grebenar and Pascha Gerlinger
Designed by Barry Age

Little brothers can be a lot of trouble.

My little brother doesn't have to do anything around here. *I* have to do all the work.

It's my job to feed our puppy and clean up her messes. All my little brother does is play ball with her.

I have to help wash the dishes—my little brother doesn't. Not since he dropped Dad's favorite mug.

When we visit Grandma and Grandpa,
I have to sit inside with the grown-ups while
my little brother plays outside with
Grandma's ducks.

But when the ducks get out of the yard, *I'm* the one who has to round them up and chase them home.

My little brother is always messing with my stuff.

Like the time he used my new baseball glove and left it in the yard.

Or the time he played with my train and crashed it onto the floor.

"Sorry," he told me. "Accident."

Or when I found my bicycle tipped over—
with a dent in the fender.
"I think it was probably the wind," he said.
But I know he thinks he's too big for his tricycle.

And then there was that day I couldn't find
my favorite blue shirt ... because my brother
was wearing it!

"He wants to look like you," Mom said.
I guess he does look like me, sort of.

But sometimes my little brother is not
so bad.

When we go fishing, he finds the fattest
worms.

When our puppy, Jenny, got sick, he stayed up with me to take care of her.

And when I fell and bumped my head, he
helped Dad deliver the newspapers for my
paper route—

even though it took all afternoon.

This morning, as I was leaving for summer camp, my little brother grabbed my sleeve and wouldn't let go ...

... until I said he could take care of my things
for me.

"You can play with my train," I told him.
"And you can ride my bike. And take Jenny for
a walk."

He didn't say anything, but he let go and
waved good-bye.

That's my little brother.
You know, I might even miss him.